SUPER RABBIT BOY VS. SUPER RABBIT BOSS!

READ MORE
PRESS START!
BOOKS!

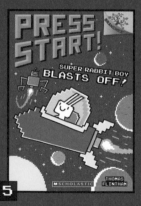

MORE BOOKS COMING SOON!

PRESS START!

SUPER RABBIT BOY VS. SUPER RABBIT BOSS!

THOMAS FLINTHAM

BRANCHES

SCHOLASTIC INC.

FOR BELLA AND TED

Copyright © 2018 by Thomas Flintham

Library of Congress Cataloging-in-Publication Data

Names: Flintham, Thomas, author, illustrator.
Title: Super Rabbit Boy vs. Super Rabbit Boss! / by Thomas Flintham.
Other titles: Super Rabbit Boy versus Super Rabbit Boss
Description: First edition. | New York : Branches/Scholastic Inc., 2018. |
Series: Press start! | Summary: Super Rabbit Boy falls down a pipe and
discovers himself in a mirror reality where everyone good is now evil,
including his mirror self, Super Rabbit Boss, and he must make friends
with King Viking (now one of the good guys) and somehow defeat his alter
ego in order to save this world—and somehow find a way back to his own reality.
Identifiers: LCCN 2017033592| ISBN 9781338034752 (pbk.) | ISBN 9781338034769 (bound library edition)
Subjects: LCSH: Superheroes—Juvenile fiction. | Supervillains—Juvenile
fiction. | Animals—Juvenile fiction. | Identity (Psychology)—Juvenile
fiction. | Video games—Juvenile fiction. | CYAC: Superheroes—Fiction. |
Supervillains—Fiction. | Animals—Fiction. | Identity—Fiction. | Video
games—Fiction.
Classification: LCC PZ7.1.F585 Sv 2017 | DDC [Fic]—dc23 LC record available at https://lccn.loc.gov/2017033592

10 9 8 7 6 5 4   21 22

Printed in China   62
First edition, February 2018
Edited by Celia Lee
Book design by Maria Mercado

TABLE OF CONTENTS

1 PRESS START!.................. 1

2 THE SAME BUT DIFFERENT... 13

3 THE MIRROR WORLDS 19

4 INTO THE CRYSTAL CAVES... 27

5 FAST PROBLEMS............... 31

6 CHOMPY SEAS!................ 36

7 NOISE IN THE WOODS 45

8 WOOF VS. BEEP!............. 53

9 BATTLE OF THE RABBITS.... 59

10 A TEARFUL ENDING........... 66

SUPER
RABBIT
BOY LAND 2
PRESS START

SUPER FUNSTON

START
SELECT

START

SELECT

This is Animal Town. It is a happy place.
But meanie King Viking likes to attack the
town with his Robot Army.

He is causing even more trouble this
time. He has kidnapped Singing Dog again.
Plus, he has taken Simon the Hedgehog
and Celia Crocodile, too! They're trapped in
Boom Boom Factory, King Viking's home.

Don't worry! Super Rabbit Boy is here. He will save the day.

He sets out for Boom Boom Factory.

To get to Boom Boom Factory, Super Rabbit Boy must get through three levels. First, Super Rabbit Boy chases King Viking's robots out of Lovely Woods.

Then he swims across the Sunny Sea.

Next, the Creepy Caves are full of mazes! They don't slow Super Rabbit Boy down. He runs faster than ever. And he jumps on all the robots in his way.

At last, he leaves the caves. He's right in front of Boom Boom Factory.

Super Rabbit Boy searches Boom Boom
Factory for his friends.

Super Rabbit Boy steps into a room full of bolts, wrenches, and all sorts of metal parts.

This must be King Viking's workshop! It's where he builds his creations.

Super Rabbit Boy spots a strange machine in the corner. There is a large warning sign next to it.

11

Yikes! Super Rabbit Boy is in trouble!

Oh bloop! I've made a mistake!

13

After falling for a long, long time, Super Rabbit Boy sees a light.

At last! A way out.

BOING!

14

Waaahh! Am I back? This looks like the room I was in before. But something is different.

Suddenly, a robot walks into the room. He sees Super Rabbit Boy and shouts!

More robots run into the room. They all start crying when they see Super Rabbit Boy!

Super Rabbit Boy is surprised.

The robots are confused. Then one steps forward.

One of the blue robots smiles and turns to the other robots.

3 THE MIRROR WORLDS

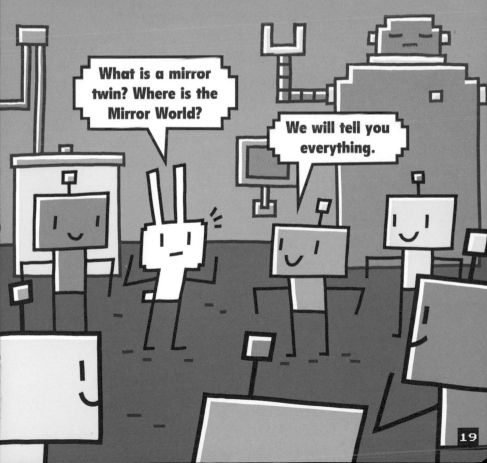

Super Rabbit Boy is very confused.

What is a mirror twin? Where is the Mirror World?

We will tell you everything.

All the robots burst into tears again!

The robots explain that Super Rabbit Boss wants their whole world to be mean and horrible. Good King Viking always does nice things, so Super Rabbit Boss captured him. He is a prisoner in Carrot Castle.

We want to rescue him, but we are scared!

26

4 INTO THE CRYSTAL CAVES

To get to Carrot Castle, Super Rabbit Boy must get through three levels. First, Super Rabbit Boy and the robots head toward the Crystal Caves.

The Crystal Caves are much nicer than the Creepy Caves in Super Rabbit Boy's world.

These caves are so pretty! In my world, they are dark and scary!

We love these caves!

The crystals make great presents!

The Crystal Caves are pretty, but they are still full of mazes.

Super Rabbit Boy follows the robots all the way through the caves to the exit.

The robots burst into tears. Simon the Horrible Hedgehog runs in circles around the group. He's very fast! How will they stop him?

The robots are busy crying. But Super Rabbit Boy is busy thinking.

Super Rabbit Boy makes all the robots stand in a circle. They extend their arms in front of them.

When I shout "GO," everyone grab. One of you should be able to catch Simon!

1. 2. 3. GO!

The robots grab at the same time. One
of the robots catches Simon the Horrible
Hedgehog!

Super Rabbit Boy and the robots tie up Simon the Horrible Hedgehog. They head out the exit.

6 CHOMPY SEAS

The <u>Stormy</u> Sea lies ahead of the group. It looks very gloomy.

> The **<u>Sunny</u> Sea** in my world is much nicer! Can you robots swim?

> We can! Good King Viking made us out of very rare waterproof parts.

A big, scary crocodile bursts from the sea!
The robots start to cry.

How will Super Rabbit Boy and the robots defeat Celia the Crunching Crocodile?

Super Rabbit Boy has an idea!

Robots, can you build things? Can you build a super strong boat?

We can build anything!

We can use these crystals from the caves!

They will make our boat strong!

The robots start building. They're very fast!

The crystal boat is ready. It looks really strong. But is it strong enough to beat Celia and her crunching crocodile teeth?

The boat sails into the Stormy Sea. Celia is not happy.

Celia swims straight toward the crystal boat!

Celia swoops in and bites the side of the boat.

CRUNCH!

Super Rabbit Boy checks the side of the boat. Is it okay?

The boat is fine! But Celia's crunching crocodile teeth are not. They are broken!

Hooray! We're safe!

Waaaaa!

It is Celia's turn to cry!

The crystal boat sails smoothly past the crying crocodile.

The sea is stormy, but the crystal boat is strong and fast. Soon they see land!

Super Rabbit Boy and the robots jump
onto the shore.

They are close to Carrot Castle. But the
Weird Woods stand in their way. They are
not like the Lovely Woods. They look spooky!
The robots start to cry.

The robots are scared, but they follow Super Rabbit Boy into the woods. They are still crying.

Suddenly, a loud noise shakes the whole woods!

The robots cry even more!

BEEP! BOOP!

BOOP! BEEP!

What was that?

IT WAS ME —

Shouting Dog lets out a super loud bark. The bark is so powerful that it blows Super Rabbit Boy and the robots back to the shore.

His voice doesn't sound as nice as **Singing Dog!**

Oh boop!

What a scary sound!

Super Rabbit Boy and the robots know what to do! They get right to work. They walk back into the woods. Shouting Dog finds them, but they are ready.

Shouting Dog starts barking, but the robots are not scared. They've built a giant megaphone with the boat's crystals! They all shout into it!

Keep going, robots! You can do it!

Shouting Dog is loud, but the robots are louder! They blast him backward.

He is blasted far, far away.

Look out, Super Rabbit Boss! Super Rabbit Boy and the robots are on the way!

Super Rabbit Boy and the robots arrive at Carrot Castle.

Boing! Boing! Here we are!

Oh beep!

Oh boop!

This Carrot Castle is much creepier than the Carrot Castle in Super Rabbit Boy's world.

The robots spot Good King Viking in a cage. Super Rabbit Boss springs into action! What is his plan?

Super Rabbit Boss puts on a giant
Robo-Rabbit Robot Suit!

The robots start to cry.

Super Rabbit Boss grabs Super Rabbit Boy.

The robots start to cry even more! Is this game over for Super Rabbit Boy?

10 A TEARFUL ENDING

The robots keep crying and crying. Soon, the room starts to fill with their tears. Suddenly, Super Rabbit Boy remembers something.

Hey, robots! You really are terrible!

He is right!

We are rotten robots!

The robots cry harder. Super Rabbit Boss
dances and splashes around with joy.

The Robo-Rabbit Robot Suit starts to shake and spark.

The robo-suit explodes!

The blast sends Super Rabbit Boss flying through the roof of Carrot Castle.

Good King Viking is free!

Super Rabbit Boy gets ready to go back to his world. Good King Viking gives him a present.

This should help you handle your King Viking!

Good-bye! And remember: When you work together, you always win!

We will!

Bye boop!

Bye beep!

Soon, Super Rabbit Boy is back in his world. King Viking is waiting for him.

Super Rabbit Boy opens the present! A jet of water shoots at King Viking's robo-suit!

The robo-suit explodes. The blast sends King Viking flying! Super Rabbit Boy's friends are free!

THOMAS FLINTHAM

has always loved to draw and tell stories, and now that is his job! He grew up in Lincoln, England, and studied illustration in Camberwell, London. He now lives by the sea with his wife, Bethany, in Cornwall.

Thomas is the creator of THOMAS FLINTHAM'S BOOK OF MAZES AND PUZZLES and many other books for kids. PRESS START! is his first early chapter book series.

Can you spot the 22 differences?

PRESS START!

How much do you know about

SUPER RABBIT BOY VS. SUPER RABBIT BOSS!?

Look at pages 8 and 9 and 14 and 15. How are the rooms similar and different?

What is the Mirror World?

Why do the robots think Super Rabbit Boy is Super Rabbit Boss?

How do Super Rabbit Boy and the robots use the crystals in their adventure?

 Would you want to have a mirror twin? Why or why not? Use words and pictures to explain your answer.

scholastic.com/branches